especially for

....

with love from

....

D1511996

To my lovely adventurers,

Lucy and Nora.

May you never lose the wonder in your souls.

HAND TO HOLD

Copyright © 2021 by JJ Heller with permission by Stone Table Records Inc.
Illustrations copyright © 2021 by Alyssa Petersen

Published in the United States by WaterBrook, an imprint of Random
House, a division of Penguin Random House LLC.

WATERBROOK® and its deer colophon are registered
trademarks of Penguin Random House LLC.

Portions of text are adapted from the song "Hand to Hold" by JJ Heller, David Heller, and
Andy Gullahorn. Copyright © 2018 Butter Lid Publishing (ASCAP) & The Gullahorns Music (ASCAP).

Hardcover ISBN 978-0-593-19325-9
eBook ISBN 978-0-593-19326-6

The Library of Congress catalog record is available at https://lccn.loc.gov/2020032225.

Printed in the United States of America

waterbrookmultnomah.com

10 9 8 7 6 5 4 3 2 1

First Edition

Book and cover design by Sonia Persad
Cover illustrations by Alyssa Petersen

SPECIAL SALES Most WaterBrook books are available at special quantity discounts
when purchased in bulk by corporations, organizations, and special-interest groups.
Custom imprinting or excerpting can also be done to fit special needs. For information,
please email specialmarketscms@penguinrandomhouse.com.

Hand TO Hold

written by
JJ Heller

illustrated by
Alyssa Petersen

WATERBROOK

Trees are made for climbing.
Days are made for sun.

Puddles are for jumping.
Fields are made to run.

Stars are made for counting
and for wishes coming true.
Sleep is made for dreaming,

and I have dreams for you.

Stones are made
for skipping.
Stories are to tell.

Life is made for living.
I pray you
live it well.

Learning comes from trying,
so don't be afraid to lose.

Songs are made for singing.

I'll sing this one for you . . .

May you never lose the
wonder in your soul.
May you always have
a blanket for the cold.

May the living light
inside you
be the compass
as you go.

May you always know you have my hand to hold.

The longest days of summer
are for flying with your kite

and spinning through the sprinklers
until fireflies dance at night.

The painted days
of autumn are for
pies and pumpkins too

and watching
the leaves falling
like I've fallen for you.

When winter,
    like a whisper,
wraps up the world
    in white,

you warm my heart with laughter
when we have snowball fights.

As cold melts into springtime,

the blossoms burst and bloom.

Each flower is a treasure,

just as I treasure you.

May you never lose the
wonder in your soul.
May you always have
a blanket for the cold.

May the living light
inside you
be the compass
as you go.

May you always know
you have my hand to hold.

You help me find the magic in ordinary days.

Each minute is a marvel.

No moment is the same.

You notice every sunset, reminding me what's true.

You're full of awe and wonder,

and I'm in awe of you.

My darling, you are priceless, and I am deeply blessed
to hug you in the evening and tuck you into bed.

Let's bow our heads together
before this day is through.
God hears us when we're praying,
so I'll pray over you . . .

May the good Lord bless and keep you
and fill you with his peace.

His face will shine upon you even as you sleep.

Every day you're changing. Sometimes I wish it wasn't true.

Hearts are made for giving. I've given mine to you.

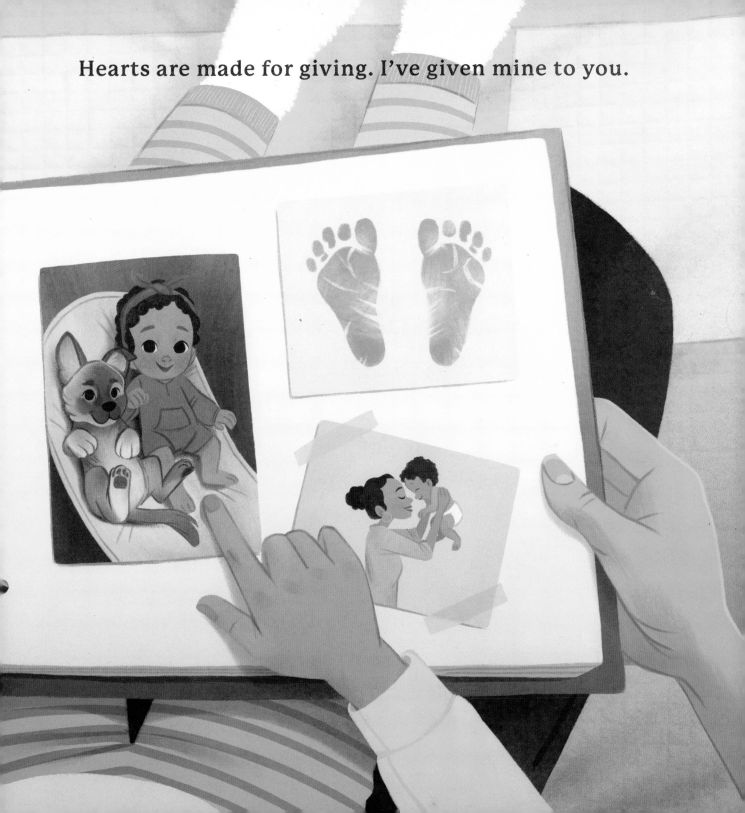

May you never lose the
wonder in your soul.

May you always have a
blanket for the cold.

May the living light
inside you be the
compass as you go.

May you always know
you have my hand to hold.

Big Dipper